The Biggest Popcorn Party Ever in Center County

Jane Hoober Peifer

Photographs by Marilyn Peifer Nolt

HERALD PRESS
Scottdale, Pennsylvania
Kitchener, Ontario

1987

Library of Congress Cataloging-in-Publication Data

Peifer, Jane Hoober, 1953-
  The biggest popcorn party ever.

  Summary: Previously reluctant to share their
popcorn crop with friends, a barn fire pops Henry
and Martha's stored kernels and they decide to
have the grandest party ever.
  [1. Popcorn—Fiction. 2. Sharing—Fiction]
I. Nolt, Marilyn Peifer, ill. II. Title.
PZ7.P3585Bi   1987   [E]   86-27063
ISBN 0-8361-3435-4 (pbk.)

THE BIGGEST POPCORN PARTY EVER IN CENTER COUNTY
Copyright © 1987 by Herald Press, Scottdale, Pa. 15683
  Published simultaneously in Canada by Herald Press,
  Kitchener, Ont. N2G 4M5. All rights reserved.
Library of Congress Catalog Card Number: 86-27063
International Standard Book Number: 0-8361-3435-4
Printed in the United States of America
Design by Ann Graber/Paula Johnson

92 91 90 89 88 87 10 9 8 7 6 5 4 3 2 1

Special thanks—

*To Ellen for sharing
her popcorn dreams,*

*To Dick and Wanda
for sharing their farm.*

Henry Huffnagel grew the best popcorn in Center County. Year after year, he carefully prepared the soil, planted the seed, cultivated the rows, and harvested the crop.

It was hard work, but Henry liked to work. He was always anxious to see what the good soil would produce. He lived with a sparkle in his eye.

Martha Huffnagel was his wife. She took life seriously and worked hard keeping the farm in tip-top shape.

She was proud of their popular popcorn, and made sure that each kernel was properly cared for and harvested.

One evening after supper, Henry settled into his porch chair. He put his head back, closed his eyes, and thought about how much fun it would be to share this bumper crop of popcorn with their friends.

"Martha," he said quietly, "I was just thinking.... Wouldn't it be fun to have a big popcorn party after harvest?"

"Henry, I can't understand you," Martha replied sternly. "We work hard. We grow the best popcorn in Center County. We deserve all the money we get by *selling* the popcorn."

Aw, I know, Martha. I was just thinking. By the way, did you see that cup of popcorn on the counter? I shelled a cob today out in the field to see how it is doing. Could we pop that right now?"

"You go ahead, Henry. I'm tired. I'm going to bed," answered Martha.

So Henry popped a small bowl of popcorn for himself. Each snow white kernel squeaked against his teeth and then crunched as he savored the delicious flavor.

"It would be really fun to share the popcorn with our friends," he mused.

Later that week, when the harvest was in, and all the popcorn was waiting in bins in the barn, Henry sank back into his rocking chair and sighed. "Another good harvest, Martha."

"Well, I should hope so," replied Martha. "We sure have worked hard enough."

"God has been good to us once again. I wish. . . ." Henry stopped himself and returned to his newspaper. He knew how Martha felt.

It was Saturday night. Early Monday morning the trucks would come to begin unloading the bins of popcorn. He'd better get a good night's sleep.

On Sunday morning, Henry and Martha went to church in town with their friends and neighbors. Pastor Taylor greeted them at the door. "Good morning, Mr. Huffnagel. I saw your corn picker in the field this week. Have you had another good harvest?"

"Yes, and we are grateful, Pastor Taylor," said Henry.

"Hard work, though," added Martha.

"I'm sure it was," replied Pastor Taylor.

After the congregation sang a song, Pastor Taylor spoke. "I will be reading from 1 Timothy 6, verse 18," he said. " 'Command them to do good, to be rich in good deeds, and to be generous and willing to share.' "

Sunday afternoon, after a delicious dinner, Henry and Martha sat down in the living room. Even before Martha had done three stitches on her crocheting, Henry was snoring.

"I am glad he can rest, now that the harvest is in," she thought. "Tomorrow will be another big day.

"I'll feel better when those trucks are loaded and on their way. There are plenty of things around here that could use some improvement. Maybe Henry and I will even take a little vacation this winter."

Some time later, Martha walked into the kitchen to get a drink of water. As she glanced toward the barn, she saw snow.

Snow? But wait. Was it snow? In October? It couldn't be snow!

She looked again. It was popcorn! Popcorn was shooting from the barn windows. The ground was getting white as it piled up around the barn.

Oh, my! Oh, my goodness!" shouted Martha. "Henry, Henry, wake up! The popcorn is popping! The popcorn is popping, Henry!"

"What did you say, Martha?" yawned Henry.

"Henry come quick. The popcorn is popping!" Martha shouted.

Henry hurried to the kitchen window and looked toward the barn. He was stunned. Popcorn was now bulging the barn doors and popcorn was visible through the top windows.

"Fire, Martha. There must be a fire! Call the fire department. Hurry!"

The fire engine sped up the lane toward the barn. The fire fighters jumped off the truck pulling their hoses. As they circled the barn, someone called, "Hold on. Don't start the water yet!"

There were no flames. The popcorn had smothered the fire. There was a faint scent of smoke, but above all there was an overwhelming smell of freshly popped popcorn—the best popcorn in Center County.

Henry and Martha stood there looking at the snowlike mounds of popcorn surrounding the barn.

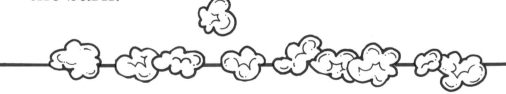

As they turned and walked toward the house, there was a long silence. "Henry," Martha said, "What are we going to do? All of the popcorn is popped. Nothing is left."

"And it happened so quickly," added Henry.

Sadly Martha said, "I guess that puts an end to any vacation plans for this winter."

"Well, Martha, I suppose it does," said Henry. Pastor Taylor's words ran through his mind: "Be generous and willing to share."

"At least, Martha, we still have the barn and the equipment to try again next year," he said.

All at once Martha stopped and faced Henry. "You know . . . we have here all that we need for a big party—the biggest party Center County has ever known."

"Oh, Martha, do you mean now . . . here . . . today?" Henry stuttered. "Are you sure?"

"Yes, I mean today," Martha answered excitedly. "Call our friends—all our friends, and *their* friends. We'll have a dandy party."

Martha scurried into the house and began looking in the pantry for bowls and cups. Henry called Rhoda, Vera and Clyde, and Pastor Taylor at the church and told them to invite everyone from town.

After Henry hung up the phone, he thought he heard Martha humming as she flitted around the kitchen preparing some lemonade. "Martha," he teased, "do I see a twinkle in your eye?"

"Oh, Henry—now go and round up some chairs. They'll soon be coming."

And so it was that Henry and Martha Huffnagel had the biggest popcorn party ever in Center County.

Left to right: Author Jane H. Peifer, Martha and Henry Huffnagel, and photographer Marilyn Nolt.

The Author

A native of Lancaster, Pennsylvania, Jane Hoober Peifer earned her B.A. in elementary education at Eastern Mennonite College, Harrisonburg, Virginia.

She and her husband served two years in Mennonite Voluntary Service in Corning, New York. While there, Jane taught remedial reading in the public school system.

Presently, she works part-time as a preschool and a private piano teacher. The Peifers attend St. Paul's United Methodist Church in Odessa, Delaware.

Jane and her husband, Daryl, are the parents of Rebecca (1978) and Andrew (1980).

The Photographer

Marilyn Nolt and husband, Larry, live in Harrisonburg, Virginia. They are the parents of Brad, Jill, and Todd.

Marilyn is an art major at James Madison University. A free-lance photographer, her work appears widely in professional journals, brochures, and religious publications.

Marilyn and Jane, her sister-in-law, collaborated on three previous picture storybooks: *Good Thoughts at Bedtime, Good Thoughts About Me,* and *Good Thoughts About People* (Herald Press, 1985).